Condor Cliff

Michèle Laframboise

Condor Cliff

A Lady Byrd Adventure

A Bold and Birding
story

Cover Design: Echofictions
Cover photographs by Krakenimages / Nina B. / Shutterstock
Author photograph by Gilles Gagnon
Interior illustration by author

This book published by :
Echofictions
Mississauga, Ontario

www.echofictions.com

ISBN 978-1-988339-08-5 (print)

Table of Contents

Dedication	vii
Condor Cliff	
Chapter 1	1
Chapter 2	3
Chapter 3	7
Chapter 4	13
Chapter 5	19
Chapter 6	23
Chapter 7	27
Chapter 8	33
Chapter 9	39
Postface	41
Heartfelt Thanks	44
About the Author	45
Other books by Michèle	47
Friends' List	49
Yearning for more stories?	50

For my grandmother
Edmée Laframboise, born Saintonge,

who introduced me to mystery novels

1

THE BEDROCK GLEAMED like the copper pans on Grandma's counter.

In the pan's bottom, the lake emerged like a turquoise tongue from the sandstone cliffs. The only sounds heard at this early hour were the gentle rolling of sand grains on the slopes, a few calls by the desert birds, and the awed murmurs of fellow tourists.

Standing by the lake near the guide, I waited for the slanting rays to touch the sandstone wall, projecting its ragged outline against the other face of the canyon. Most people saw an Amerindian's profile reflected in the lake, as the travel brochure proclaimed.

The moment came and went, without me being able to make anything out of a ragged line. I breathed an arid lungful of air, tainted with the scent of blooming flowers, of sand and mud. I walked on the ribbon-like layers of hard and soft stones. Those orange, brown and ochre ribbons crept everywhere on the canyon, as if a giant brush had painted its walls.

According to the brochure I forgot in the bus, this pool was the most beautiful place on Earth.

What good is standing in all this beauty if I cannot share it?

I came here because I had promised Paul I would.

2

MY BACKPACK AND I had stepped out of the intercity bus at the park entrance, in front of a souvenir shop offering bad coffee and no washroom.

A fast-food chain joint stood a few steps away. A quick glance around told me this was the sole eating place in the hundred or so square kilometers of the park, a valley run through by a lazy stream, riddled with paths of various lengths.

The joint's front door sucked in the drained, thirsty or (in my case) bladder-bursting passengers. I did not envy the waitress' job, as she hurried like a black-haired bird to serve every one.

Being the last out of the bus, I took my time, using my scarf to dab water on my face, and refilling my water bottle. When I finally sat at a Formica table near the kitchen, most of the tourists were eating.

Sipping a cup of freshly brewed coffee, I unfolded the map bought from the souvenir shop. I had a name scrawled on a folded mustard-yellow hospital paper.

The weary waitress brought my light salad and heavy burger. I showed her the paper. She squinted as she peered at it, thin lines fanning from her dark eyes.

"Round Lake?"

"It's a lake around here," I said, as I was hastily pushing the map away from the plates she had set down. "It would be in a narrow canyon, not like this big valley."

Her weary eyes suddenly lit.

"Oh, I see! You must mean, Bowl Lake. It's right there!"

She laid a clipped nail on the half folded map. I sighed. It was a distance I was unfit to walk.

The waitress must have guessed my dismay. She gestured to the window, pointing towards a stand of grey wood near the entrance, as big as a motel room without the motel. Secret Canyon Tours, the board said, with the operating hours.

"Hey, Lucy!" a voice called near me, "how about a nice cup of coffee?"

The waitress winced. She turned to speaking to a fortyish, stylish guy in a beige suit seated in a bench across from me.

"If you can pay for it," she said.

"Aaw, c'mon, Luce!" the stylish man said in a grating voice. "You know I've got money enough."

"Art, I can't make an exception," the harried waitress said. "This joint takes cash, and you're hogging a vacant table. If you want credit, there's the casino!"

She spoke in a low, harried voice. She knew, and obviously disliked, that patron, but couldn't show her feelings. And, somehow, she couldn't throw him out to enforce the rule of table occupancy.

"Naah, Luce, don't worry, I will have the money to pay."

Calls were coming left and right. The waitress shoulders slumped.

"Okay," she said, her voice dragging a ball of cast iron.

"For this time only, Art."

I didn't usually eavesdrop on conversations, but I checked my wallet. The stylish guy got up and left, without my hearing the familiar clink of quarters on the table. He had left without even tipping her.

Later, having making sure to leave a nice tip to the waitress, I walked thought the shops, bought a cap with the Park's logo on it, and headed to the motel-room-sized shop. A billboard announced the Bowl Lake Secret Canyon Tour, and a map printed directly on a wooden slab at the entrance showed the route to the place, passing the interstate near the county's limit.

I was pondering which birds would dwell in that narrow canyon with the blue pond.

"You're late for the evening tour, but tomorrow morning's the best time."

The stylish restaurant man rounded the motel-like counter, in his beige suit of ultra light fabric. His pointy shoes looked unsuitable for walking. To compensate for the suit, he sported a two-day beard aiming to project an outdoors rugged look, and failing.

I purchased a ticket for an early morning tour. It took some time as Art ("just call me Art"), showing teeth too perfect to be true, tried to get me to combine my ticket with a reduced Casino Tour.

"They have the best facilities for, hum, distinguished ladies like you," he said, showing more red gums and white teeth.

I was sure the Casino did have facilities for diminished ladies, but gambling was not on my bucket list.

Art accepted only cash, which irked me.

The small change he returned would have paid nicely for his coffee cup, which irked me more.

❧

I SLEPT IN A RUN-DOWN MOTEL at the edge of the small town, facing the unblinking stare of the Casino.

The town did not offered much in terms of entertainment for a distinguished lady preferring tea rooms and gardens to strip clubs and taverns. The town was dying, and the flashing casino was only one symptom among many others.

My room's thin windowpanes let in all the drunken hollering, the casino muzak, the whistles and cat calls and screeching tires, followed closely by the (sole) police car's sirens.

I didn't envy the Sheriff.

❧

THE NEXT DAY, AT DAWN, Art, neat-dressed as yesterday, greeted me along with a dozen other travelers.

He led us and our paper coffee cups to a rickety bus with the green letters Secret Canyon Tours glued on the sides. He presented himself as the discoverer of Bowl Lake. He may or may not have presented the guide accompanying us; I was too lost in my thoughts to remember. This remote canyon had once been too difficult to reach; nowadays, said Art, a lift could lower a handful of tourists at the time near the lake.

A mechanical pulley with a cement counter weight helped with the movement; Art had manned the lift with all of us in two loads. Each time, the guide supervised the exiting and the lifting off.

My own palms were white from clutching at the rail.

In my head, I still heard Paul's warm gravelly voice telling me the wonders of his childhood's secret spot.

It's the most beautiful place on Earth, Amy…

3

COLD DROPS ON MY BARE SHINS and loud splashes made me back away from the lake. A couple of the youngest travelers were testing the water, blurring the beautiful reflection of the cliff. Some other guys waded in, ogling the girls.

Those organized excursions were golden occasions for bachelors to wade into a new relation. Fortunately, my ripe age spared me most of their attentions.

A dark shadow crossed the wrinkled rock, along with a whoosh of displaced air, like those ultra light planes my niece piloted.

My head whipped up up by reflex.

Against the stark blue sky, a black shape soared, immense black wings stretched with too many fingers at the ends. Not an ULM. I noted the pink head jutting out of a fluffed collar, the white triangle under the wings. As an avid birder, I recognized a California condor.

The condor disappeared over the cliff before I could wrestle my binoculars out of their pouch. I cranked my neck, hoping to see the majestic bird make another pass.

"What was that?" a raspy voice asked.

I started.

"You spooked me!"

The guide stepped back.

"I'm sorry", he said. "It's just that I heard a noise overhead."

The man had a brooding, intelligent face, with an earthy complexion, cheekbones and black hair that spoke First Nation. His dark eyes gleamed under the rim of his reddish hat.

The hat told me than he took the scorching heat seriously, not like the tourists with baseball caps and glowing red ears. Paul had warned me from his bed about the treacherous heat. My own white "fearless explorer lady" hat had protected me through endless cruises.

"Did you see what it was?" the guide asked.

I tugged at the cord preventing said hat to fly away.

"Yes. A condor."

The guide looked up, holding his hat in place with a knobby hand. I noted the tied-up ponytail. His shirt smelled like tobacco and fabric softener, taut around the shoulders. He was well-built, but not overly muscled like all those jocks sweating in gyms. His body looked hardened by endless hours of outdoor work. (Not that I have anything against gyms: my computer-driven second nephew would have become a couch potato without those.)

"There aren't many of them around", he said.

"I don't have my Sibley with me, but you can't miss the collar and pink head".

My faithful but hefty *Sibley Guide to Birds* had been left in my locked motel room, along with my backpack. I only had a fanny pack with me, just big enough for a bottle of water and a pair of garden gloves. My compact 9x25 binoculars waited for their fifteen minutes of fame inside my cargo pant's side pocket.

"Those birds were almost extinct," he said.

The California condor had been counted as almost extinct in the '80s, from hunting and lead poisoning. They had been bred in zoos, then reintroduced in the Grand Canyon area in the 1990s. But even now, they ingested their load of lead with each bullet-riddled cadaver they found.

"They can fly over a long distance to feed", I said.

A flurry of splashes and loud whoops told me the rest of the group was enjoying the water.

I looked around for a likely place to sit, as far from the lake as I could. The wrinkled rock was uncomfortable, but I felt grateful for the sturdy cargo pants Paul had insisted I bought for our twenty-fifth anniversary trip.

"You don't swim?"

"No. Haven't even brought a suit."

There was no point in exhibiting my worn body. Paul had considered me beautiful and told me a zillion times; I didn't want to shatter this illusion.

The guide lowered himself beside me. His knee joints cracked. He gazed at the lake and the cliff, ignoring the swimmers. Some had exited the water and reclined in a shady patch, over bright colored blankets.

"The sun's still low," he said. "We have until ten. After ten, the sun will bake this place."

"Do you live around here?"

"In the village, about ten minutes north."

He looked at me. "I'm surprised you're not taking pictures."

I cupped the bulge in my pants pocket, where the binoculars rested.

"I came here more as a pilgrimage," I said.

"Why?"

My fingers traced the orange and yellow ridges in the rock.

"My husband used to live in the area when he was a boy. He came to this lake."

The man's brows rose under his hat.

"No kidding? Which tribe was he?"

I shrugged.

"None," I said. "Paul and I were two white cookies."

"But how could he have known about Bowl Lake?"

"His parents operated a fishing store on the Columbia. As a boy, he was running all over the place. He and his buddies eventually found this lake. They had dubbed it Round Lake. They kept it a secret."

The guide let out a low chuckle.

"It's certainly not a secret now!"

"I guess one of his friends eventually told someone."

"Not him?"

"No. Paul was true to his word. He only told me about it last year."

The guide smiled, adding thin creases around his lips.

"What decided him to spill the beans?"

I sighed. His detective-novel banter was lost on me.

Better to keep it short.

"He was dying."

~

At that point, I braced myself for the empty "Sorry for your loss", "our sympathies" or "By gully, so surry!"

He opened his mouth to say it, paused, then expelled a gust of air. Maybe something in my body stance had warned him against blabbing.

"So here you are", he said.

"And you, guiding tours."

He looked at the blue expanse of sky over the cliff's edge. No condor passed. His hands clenched into fists, then relaxed. Something was troubling him.

He was not the only one able to read body language.

"Would you have preferred the Lake to stay hidden?" I asked.

Will all the tech and Google maps and satellites, there was no such thing as a hidden place. Except, maybe, the deepest caves.

"Can't say I don't appreciate the business, but still..."

His double negative sentence was left unfinished.

I made a rapid tally in my head. "You get what, a dozen tourists down here, one, two times per day?

"Only mornings and evenings."

I had forgotten the shop's schedule. It made sense, considering the intolerable heat.

"So, at the fee you charged per head, it makes for a good living, I would say."

The man zipped open a side pocket and brought out a notebook, the cover worn smooth. He looked into it and smiled.

"You're good with numbers."

"I did some bookkeeping in my time."

"I ain't that good in math. Art's the one doing the numbers for the company."

"You could really make a better living than ferrying out tourists here."

He looked away. Something was gnawing at him.

Now, the whoops were getting louder as sun beams touched the cliff over the lake. The tour was supposed to last one more hour.

I stood up, slowly, to compare the place to what Paul had told me about it.

The canyon followed an East-West curve, with Bowl Lake bulging from the middle of the arc.

The western side of the canyon curled beyond the lake to taper into a narrow pass. At winter's end, the constrained water rose before hurtling downward a sixty feet drop, in a wider canyon. The waterfall pictures, shot from the other side, showed a blend, featureless "exit" cliff that prevented any attempt at climbing. Paul had had to scramble by another route to get in.

I walked away from the lake.

The lift was about fifty meters up the well-packed trail, hidden by the jutting Amerindian's profile.

Rounding the ragged edge, I passed the wooden platform, sitting idly a few feet from the rocky wall, taut cables at the ready. A bright orange toilet stall, a necessity of civilisation, huddled in a recess.

The cliff had no eroded hollow nor sharp protrusions. It was so comic-book-straight that I almost looked up for Will-E Coyote.

4

I TRUDGED TOWARD THE LOWEST PART of the canyon, choosing my steps carefully along the now dried-out stream. Those ochre and orange ridges, as artistic as they looked on the National Geographic photographs, were tricky to negotiate. I pictured a very young Paul, climbing down the cliff by his own means, using the harder ridges as handholds.

Two turns later, the cries and laughter fell away as in a dream. I stood still, unfolding the field glasses, listening.

A cascading suite of clear whistles rose from a nearby niche, maybe twenty feet over me. A rock wren! Paul had often evoked its heart-warming song.

I immerse myself in the beauty my husband had discovered as a boy.

My breath caught.

Oh, Paul!

It still felt like yesterday I was holding his hand for the last time. It has been already one year since my husband, so strong, had been defeated by a bunch of rogue cells.

My vision blurred.

I blinked and lift up my eyes, but the light-brown bird stayed as low-profile as its song wasn't. Wrens were notoriously difficult to spot, especially in a rocky setting reproducing their colors.

There might be nests up there, among the dried-up herbs and roots. The ridges were like long stairs, and some wide enough to step on. So, I ascended the slope, until the angle became too steep. Then, I followed a wider ridge, like a level line on a topographic map.

The walls closed on me. The ridge got more slippery with birds droppings, caked dust, dried out mud from the spring rains.

Few flowers grew on the dirt gathered on the ridge. A few meager willows tried to root in the scattered rocks, a struggle they were about to lose.

I was scanning the opposite wall surface, when a rock came loose under my left shoe. I reached out to stabilise myself, but a stray branch from a soon-to-be-dead pine snagged on the flap of my waist pack and I lost my balance.

I fell like a boulder, dislodging more rocks.

A dried out bush tampered my fall, the shock chasing off the air from my lungs. More rubble fell as quick steps hurried towards me. Two big arms yanked me on my feet. I looked up in a pair of dark brown eyes.

"Heavens, lady! Are you OK? I should have kept up with you."

"You followed me?"

"Couldn't let a client fall to her death on my watch."

His humor fell on deaf ears. So what if I had fallen to my death?

I recognized the downer thought as soon as it whipped my brain. Those exertions had winded me down. I needed to rest.

I found found a wide enough ridge and sat on it, the guide lowering himself beside me. Our position overlooked the low V of the exit fall, a narrow doorway. There was no fall. The little stream had dried up there, as the Lake itself would, later in the season.

But for now, a gentle breeze swished by, from the outer wall, carrying fresh air. I took two slow gulps of lukewarm water from my bottle.

"Are you better?"

His tone held a nugget of kindness at odd with his rugged features.

I didn't know his name. He didn't wear a name tag nor did he volunteer that information. Somehow, I didn't care to appear too frail in front of this outdoor man.

"Yes, yes!" I said. "I do walk a lot, you know, but I'm more used to level grounds. And I trekked to many places with my husband..."

My throat closed, as a flurry of memories rose.

Paul clinging with one hand to a tree branch a feet in the air over a precipice, posing an elusive bunting. Paul wading in murky amazonian waters, defying deadly piranhas and more deadly bacterias, to capture a flight of red and green aras. Paul across me, at a bamboo table lit by candles, surrounded by the music of mosquitoes...

The canyon's wrinkles waved and blurred.

This time, I could not prevent tears from escaping. I sucked in a ragged breath, to no avail. I turned on my side and hid my face in my palms.

ॐ

TO HIS MERIT, the guide did not move closer to take advantage. He sat there, silent, waiting out the storm. I dried my eyes with my sleeve.

"You loved him."

A question and a statement in the same three words.

"Paul was… he was so strong. In every senses of the word. Physically. Morally. He was a solid oak dug deep in the shifting marsh of life."

Another minute passed. The guide shifted.

"If I may ask… How did your husband die?"

"Liver cancer."

I didn't need to say more. Silence stretched the time between us. In any other circumstances, it would have been qualified as a companionable.

A chirpy whistle rose a series of fluid kiiiit-kitsh-kitsh spiraling towards a high nasal squeal.

Not a rock wren, I thought, the birder cleanly divided from the bereaved woman. I lifted my binoculars and pointed toward the sound. Something moved: a light brown wren with the superciliary line, but sporting a big white throat. My mental repertory opted for Catherpes mexicanus, a canyon wren, well-known for colonizing narrow rock crevices.

Decades before, Paul must have heard its soothing song.

❧

THE WALK BACK TO THE LAKE was peaceful, the canyon wren's song still in my ears.

A faint swoop echoed over us. The condor was still making his rounds over the canyon.

"You should name this place Condor Canyon," I said. "Or Condor Cliff."

There was a pleasant alliteration in the former, but the latter's monosyllabic simplicity held a certain appeal.

"The two have a nice ring," he said. "Speaking of names, mine's Ed. Edward WindChaser."

A poetic name.

"Amanda Byrd", I offered.

He smiled.

About twenty minutes had elapsed since I strolled down the western part of the canyon. As we got closer to the lake, toward the faint echoes of splashing and whooping, something felt wrong. As we passed the straight cliff, I found it, and stopped.

Edward gave a gasp.

"What the…" he said, then clenched his jaw shut.

He couldn't cry out to be heard by the tourists.

The platform was as we had left it, against the cliff. With the pull cables all rolled over.

5

Ed walked slowly around the platform, then looked up to the cliff's edge.

I used my binoculars and adjusted the lenses for the vertical distance. One of the "arms" of the mechanical lift was askew, as freezed in the middle of waving goodbye.

The guide was examining the frayed end of a lift cable. The cable couldn't be that worn out in this dry climate.

"It was cut", he said, his voice drained of his previous energy.

Silence enveloped us, cut by the angry warnings of a thrush, as the word sabotage sank in.

"Who could have done this?" I asked. "A competitor in the business?"

"I… I don't know," he said, stuttering. "We don't have much competition for this place. Art borrowed the seed money and built up the company. He manages the finances."

I did not find in my heart the guts to share my personal thoughts about his boss. The slick guy had been obviously pulling hefty profits from the business, underpaying the guide.

That lift accident reeked of insurance scam, done in haste. Maybe slick Art was a casino player swimming in debts. It irked me that he would put innocent lives at risk to grab a few more dollars.

Ed took off his hat, passing a hand in his unruly hair.

"We were friends," he said as to reassure himself. "My wife and I met him while honeymooning, years ago."

Disappointment or dismay etched sad lines on his face. His gaze turned to his boots inside told me of unspoken quarrels.

Ed put back his cap. This moment of vulnerability, the fact that he had let me see it, touched me.

"This can get dangerous", he said.

"Why?"

"Past nine o'clock, the temperature will rise over one hundred Fahrenheit. At ten o'clock, it will get definitely uncomfortable, even in the shade. After eleven, the secret canyon will morph into a secret cauldron."

Not good for the older travelers among us. The desert heat took its toll, each year, on the careless. Or the hatless.

"Well, at least, there's plenty of water to drink," I said.

Ed frowned.

"That lake has stood stagnant for weeks. And guess what dwells in after hundreds of tourists have already waded in?" He gestured towards the sky. "Only that condor would find the water palatable!"

I winced, picturing that tainted water falling in my delicate stomach.

The guide took out a matte black cell phone from his pants' pocket, flipped it open. He frowned.

"No signal."

I tried the bright green hi-tech ultrathin cell my computer-savvy nephew gave me last Christmas.

No bars.

“Maybe someone else will have a phone, with another provider…” I said, helpfully.

He shook his head.

“Same problem. This canyon is too deep. And it’s too early for a satellite to catch my antenna.”

“What time is it?”

“Around eight.”

“So, for now, the visitors would not notice that we’re stuck.”

“Not unless they need to take a dump”, he said, pointing to the lonely orange stall.

I thought about Paul, exploring this place so many years ago. About what he had told me.

“Edward,” I said. “If I may be so bold, I think there is another way out”.

He shot me a puzzled look.

“Upstream,” I said.

He did not believe me.

“There nothing there,” he said, gesturing to the canyon’s East end. “Those walls close tight as an ass!”

I pursed my lips.

“Beg your pardon”, he added, suddenly conscious of his lapse.

Anxiety took its toll in different ways.

“Follow me”, I said to the guide.

6

I PRECEDED HIM past the lake and its splashing visitors, then, up the gentle slope of the eastern part.

The well-worn path uphill stopped at a point where a thorny bush and a host of baby pines made the trek very uncomfortable. Paul had been there before. I extracted a pair of gardening gloves from my small pack, to push away the pine's prickly limbs.

Gently pushing, I managed to pass through. Behind me, a muttered curse told me Ed was getting acquainted with the thorns. I plodded up on the traitorous trail, through ferns and baby pines trying to adjust to the harsh conditions, scaring away wrens and other passerines who had never in their short life encounter a biped.

The narrow couloir crept up, my shoes negotiating the angular rocks fragments accumulated by erosion.

The shadow of the condor passed us, as a silent encouragement.

We talked a little, about our families.

He had lost a cousin to liver disease a few years ago, a waking call for him to ditch alcohol. He had been sober ever since.

Ed's daughters were talented and sharp, and he hoped to give them a better life than the one he had known, having dropped out of school at the tender age of 14. His wife worked overtimes at the fast-food outlet.

"I've met her," I said, surprising myself.

The harried black-haired waitress was the right age. Art's attitude towards Luce at the restaurant took a new light.

A vain man, his advances ignored. And it explained her lack of response to Art's disregard of the restaurant's rules. She did not want to alienate her husband's boss.

I told him about my ULM gliding niece, my gym-going nephew and my own bird-watching dad. Paul always had an adventurous streak. He had taken the bird bug from me. When I mentioned his forays here, Ed told me that his older brother may have been one of Paul's native friends.

"My brother loved to roam the valleys," Ed said, venting himself with his hat. "He would disappear for days."

The path became muddier, with a dying trickle of water snaking around fallen sandstone fragments. After another ten minutes of climbing, the canyon closed abruptly. At the foot of the conjoining walls, there was a depression where a hidden spring had created a pool of pristine water, with pale yellow chalk edges marking calcareous deposits. The overflow of this pool flowed down, a small stream cascading happily before the porous rock silenced it. Did Paul hear its lovely music?

I pictured the early spring rains filling the depression, cascading down our path to fill the larger Bowl Lake, then snaking along the canyon and splashing through the narrow exit, giving away life-sustaining moisture for the sturdy plants.

Taking two steps back, I looked up. The walls over the pond formed a V of sky and striated cliffs. An experimented climber with the right gear could attempt to get to the top. Not me.

I kneeled, pulled off my gloves and dunk my hands in the water, letting the wonderful freshness creep over my sun-dappled arms. The pond was about three or four feet deep. I pictured Paul and his buddies coming upon this cool oasis under this pounding heat. He must have stopped here, to kiss the water.

I sat, exhausted from the exercise.

"Let's make a pause before going on," I said.

He checked his watch.

"It's eight thirty", he said, neither approving nor disapproving.

"Just a minute or two, please."

I shuck off my shoes and socks, then plunged my feet in the small pool. The sudden cold jolted me, but I spread my toes against the slippery rocks lining the bottom. Some people are religious in other ways. Mine was to enter feet first into communion with a body of water.

Closing my eyes, I felt Paul's presence, imagining his feet brushing mine under the surface. The canyon wren's liquid voice lifted my spirits again. My ears drank the happy kiiiit-kitsh-kitsh song again. As a seasoned birder, I knew all the facts about mating calls, territorial warnings, danger alerts hidden behind those melodious chants. It didn't take anything away from this uplifting moment.

Ed splashed some water on his face, red from the exertion.

"I never went back here after the first tourist season", he said.

He sat, his back against the vertical stone of the cliff. Behind him, a pale grey serpent was coiled.

"Ed!" I hissed, pointing.

He did not jump, which would have spooked the snake. He turned his head, slowly. Then he reached out and pulled the serpent's head to the light of day. Smiling as he did so.

It was a cord, looped upon itself, frayed and gnawed. Tears came to my eyes.

"His?" he asked.

I nodded.

Paul had told me how he convinced his buddies to lower him in the big V-cliff, using his dad's alpinist cord. He had then walked down the jumble of rocks, until he came across the blue bowl lake. When he retraced his steps from the lake, he found the other secret.

7

Drying my toes, I examined the diverging faces of the canyon. Paul had left a tell-tale sign to mark his finding.

The condor made a slow dip on the left, turning.

The carrion-eater might have a nest nearby. As my eyes followed its flight, a faded red fabric winked at me from a ledge that must have been a dozen feet over our heads when we passed under it, climbing up.

A desiccated bush hung there.

I put back shoes and gardening gloves, and got up. The ledge of hardened rock holding the bush was continuous. So I stepped gingerly on it and began shifting my feet sideways, shoes pointing toward the cliff. Ed sucked in air and got up.

"Hey, wait for me!"

The ledge was wide enough at some spots to allow me to walk, on hand trailing the soft layer. At other places, it was so narrow I had to cling in earnest to an upper hard ledge.

I heard a "Crap!" and a spattering of rocks echoing down the canyon.

Ed was hanging from the upper ledge, a large opening under his dangling feet. I gasped. A puffing laugh escaped his lips as his hat flew down.

"'Guess your husband had been a skinny lad when he walked on this ledge."

The hat landed in the path, a black dot. I held my breath as the guide's feet managed to purchase support from the rock. I release it once Ed reached me. If he had fallen and gotten badly injured, I would have had to go back alone to the group and break the bad news.

"We're almost there," I said.

I could see a shadow behind the bush with the scarf. The ledge was, thanks God, wide enough to prevent more falls.

In the softer part of the rock, a crack opened, about two feet high and three wide. I bent over, but my guide put a restraining hand on my shoulder.

"There could be snakes."

A cogent advice. Trusting my gardening gloves, I plunged head first inside.

There weren't any snakes. But, as I blocked the light from the entrance, a high-pitch alert cry rose. I had barely the time to make out two or three twigs assemblages on the floor. before loud shrieks and fluttering wings filled the passage. I bent down as low as my spine would allow, my head taking the soft beating of many wings. Behind me, Ed cursed as birds flew out.

When I dared look again, the dried grass nests were deserted, save for one with four creamy eggs with brown spots. The mother (or father, as wrens shared family tasks) had wisely elected to fly and live another day instead of sacrificing his or her life in vain. There were only two of them. Their outrage had multiplied them by twenty...

As I has thought, the floor was a harder rock layer, continuous. I skirted the empty nests, looking broken and disjoined. Those had been assembled as extras by the male, to let his companion choose. Not touching the full eggs nest, I shuffled on. After two body lengths or so, the ceiling receded. I stopped to allow my eyes to get used to the darkness.

And to the hidden secret.

"Holy..." Edward began, then expelled his breath.

A faint light coming from some hole up the roof revealed a large room, with stalactites falling like drapes on a honeymoon suite bed, met by rising stalagmites. In the center area, the stalagmites had been hacked at knee level to form low mounds. The stone floor was littered with yellowed newspapers gnawed through, bits and pieces of tools, twigs and some more empty nests. Blackened logs lay near a camp fire set directly under the hole, for ventilation.

"Here it is," I said, in a low, reverent tone.

I stopped in front of the ancient fireplace, and breathed in the dusty, calcareous, scent. By standing here, I had achieved my husband's heart's desire: we, reunited across the years in this sacred place.

Tears welled in my eyes, as I imagined teenage boys huddling together around their small fire.

All those years ago, Paul had found this kernel of happiness. He must have felt so sad to leave this place, and his friends. His father had wanted him to pursue higher studies.

And so it was that our paths crossed at the same university.

ED KNEELED CLOSE to a stalagmite mound, generating a pale dust cloud. The dust's faint organic stench told me about countless bats perched upstairs.

The guide lifted up a round object from the mound. A small, rotund clay pot decorated with wavy incisions. A trace of red lingered in the low grooves.

On the next mound, a bird lay on its side, curly feathers outlines carved in the grey wood. The head looked like a condor's, sprouting like a flower form a bulging wooden collar. Other figurines, shaped from the same dried out grey wood, mounted a silent guard around the fireplace.

"Those pots", Ed murmured. "All made from clay. The children did not bring those here with them."

"Look at those wavy motives", I said.

"Once, my grand-mother spoke to me about a hidden ritual cave."

As children, Paul and his friends did not fully realize the significance of the artifacts left there by unknown ancestors. The boys never told their parents. In this canyon, they had a secret place, away from adults.

Ed lay down the pot and stood up.

"Well, that doesn't help a lot if we can't get off the canyon. That frigging hole up there is out of reach."

That friggin' hole's light revealed rows of upside-down bats hanging under the ledges. I pursed my lips. Time to look for the prop Paul had mentioned to me, from his hospital bed.

"Here", I said, pointing to a pale column. Fine calcareous tears had solidified, building a bridge between stalactite and stalagmite. Leaning against it was a crude ladder, its wooden bars bound by netted vegetal threads.

Having accustomed my eyes, I could follow the squares of bedrock cut by the ancestors to abut the ladder's feet. A second ladder was fixed up where the first one ended. And a third one, still using the protruding layers of hard rock as support.

I grasped the first ladder with two hands. It felt solid enough. Some lighter-tone threads woven along the coarser strands told me Paul and his friends had reinforced the cord.

High overhead, daylight refracted over the rock, carrying a promise of sunshine.

I took the lead, confidant that Edward would catch me if I slipped.

The gloves helped my grip on the coarse fibers, some sticking out, hard as cactus spines. Edward was bare-handed but did not wince. Ascending the fifteen or so meters took a good ten minutes. Paul had insisted that I should test each ring before putting my full weight on it. My scared rabbit brain had insisted on going very slo-owly around the sleeping bats.

The sun glare blinded me as I emerged from a crack in the ground, along with two of three bats that Ed's larger body had unwittingly disturbed. After they had disappeared, I dusted myself, checking for bites or new scratches beside the ones from my previous fall. None.

A buzzard's harsh call echoed, far away. A light breeze chased some leaves away. I could make out, very far, the big billboard, the small stand, and the pulley's raised arms.

The shiny white bus was nowhere to be found.

Art had vanished, as those slick men usually did. Maybe an extra windfall at the casino yesterday decided him to scamper away. But it did not explain why Art would bother to sabotage the lift. Alas, twisted minds have existed as long as humanity.

I said none of this to my companion.

Ed did not lose time in speculations. He pulled out his cell. This time, he managed to pick up a signal stable enough to place a 9-1-1 call.

8

I WAITED IN THE SHADOW of the billboard as Ed lowered himself down on an extra length of rope scavenged from the upper part of the broken pulley. The other end was tied to the billboard post, under my careful watch.

I couldn't approach the edge of the cliff without quavers running up my spine. Paul had been the rock climber, not me.

There was silence, as the cord tensed and dulled between my fingers. Suddenly anguished and surprised shouts echoed off the canyon faces. Ed had made it unscathed to the bottom.

While Ed and I were securing the rope, we had decided not to mention the cave to my fellow visitors.

The older people could not reach the entrance nor climb the rickety ladder without severe risks; the hotter heads would blabber about the Indiana Jones-like treasure cave as soon as they went online.

Ed stayed with them. Soon, splashing told me that Bowl Lake acted as the sole respite from the mounting heat.

Its waters were less pristine when the rescuers reached the site.

❧

Eventually, the police managed to get everyone out of Secret Canyon which, by the time they got here, had indeed become hot as a cauldron.

All tourists had waited immersed to the neck in the now-tepid water, the relentless sun pounding on the uncovered heads. I wondered how the small rock wrens fared. Better, I'm sure.

Ed was the last one to be hauled up.

While officers and rescuers managed the older tourists, Ed stepped away from the throng, holding his phone against his ear. He was trying to reach his boss, trying to make sense of the disappearing bus, the destroyed pulley.

The Sheriff had called for another mean of transportation, his function car and the tow truck being not enough. A bus from a nearby canoe expedition company would take home the weary tourists.

I looked over my shoulder. Ed was still crunched over his phone. His fingers punched numbers. He waited, but I could guess the silence at the other end.

A low purring announced the promised transport. The group happily welcomed the bus, especially the air conditioning and washroom.

I elicited to stay, guessing that the Sheriff's car could take us back.

"Why would he do that?" Ed kept mumbling, a rhetorical question. Like me, he had come to the conclusion of an elaborate insurance scam.

The Sheriff, a hale and hearty man under his sturdy hat, came towards us.

"Well, my deputee took some pictures, and we're set. Don't worry, mister WindChaser, we'll find the scamp who did it. Care for a ride, Mister, Miss?"

As we were following the Sheriff, a swift shadow crossed ours. I lifted my head, in time to glimpse the condor gliding in the brilliant blue, false black fingers extended at the end of his wings.

"If only this bird could tell us what he saw," Ed said.

IT TURNED OUT that the condor didn't need to give us a clue.

The next day, I was sipping coffee with Ed's wife. Their little cottage sat in a remote spot of the valley, across a low reddish hill with a spatter of chandelier cactus as sentinels. From the WindChaser's porch, I had the surprise to discover no less than three wren nests among protruding slabs of sandstone.

Luce proved as witty and entertaining as I had gathered from the restaurant. She had taken a day off from the fast food outlet. We sat on the porch, appreciating the gradual cooling down from the high heat, the low hiss of sand kissed by the wind, the proud challenges of rock wrens claiming territorial supremacy, the angry cawing of a solitary crow crossing the reddening sky.

I didn't see the condor.

Ed walked in with a man about his age, who was favoring his left leg. One shoulder was lower than the other.

"Simon!" Luce said. "Come in!"

She sprang up to prepare a fuming cup for Ed's older brother. I dragged myself up more slowly from my wicker chair.

Simon had called in to talk about the past. He was bent since a work accident, but talkative. He had known Paul as a child and had taken part in the canyon expeditions. It was Simon who advised Paul, on their last day in the cave, to leave the ladders in place.

I thanked him profusely.

"Without those ladders, Ed and I would never have come back alive."

"Stranger things have happened," Simon said. "Paul told me he saw a large condor circling over the canyon when we waded in the lake. I never saw the damn bird."

I was savoring this coincidence when Luce turned up the radio.

"They found the bus!" she said.

A male gravelly anchor voice announced that the police had found a white bus in a ditch, at a secondary road.

Burnt to a crust.

With a charred body inside.

⁂

TIDBITS OF INFORMATION dripped slowly over the next day. As I was waiting for the intercity bus, a black-and-white TV bolted to the wall announced that dental records had permitted to identify the body. It was indeed Ed's boss, the elusive Art.

As the bus was speeding away, I learned from the driver's open radio that the slick man's death hadn't been an accident. Nor had he been favored by the gambling gods.

More pieces joined the puzzle after my arrival at home.

Slick Art's fate had arisen from a long pattern. While his clients were looking in awe at the Canyon, Ed's boss used to take the company's innocent tourist vehicle to smuggle hi-tech drugs across the state's borders. The company served as a front to launder the money. The money ended up sponging his gambling losses.

Art may have wanted to get off the gig, but his gains kept evaporating at the casino. This had been going on for years (so said the police), until a bigger fish in the drug runners' pond found out.

The drug lord did not take lightly to being double-crossed. The sabotage of the pulley and our resulting anguish had been an afterthought.

To provide an example.

A thought floated up my head: of that drug lord abandoned in the secret cauldron at midday, with only the condor to hear his pleas for help.

9

MONTHS LATER, I made the trip back to witness the first shoveling of earth for the future *Condor Canyon Ritual Cave* museum. The low-roofed building would be erected on the plateau, set a careful distance away from the canyon's edge. Bright orange ribbons marked the path to the upper cave opening.

The ritual place had sparked a new interest in the area. Nobody had argued about the chosen name, since "Secret Canyon" felt borrowed from a dime novel title. I would still have preferred Condor Cliff, but the mayor was adamant that the new name would attract the Californian crowd.

Edward Windchaser had taken up the business of ferrying down visitors, scholars and archeologists to the ritual cave. The new lift was a reliable contraption, compliant to both state and county's bylaws. Ed's wife now worked for him or rather, with him, greeting the visitors. His older brother manned the lift. The family's combined earnings would provide for the daughters' education.

The two girls stood erect, in traditional striped robes, a flurry of red and yellow beads erupting from their braids. The younger one smiled as the mayor made a show of huffing and puffing, shoveling more words than clods of dirt.

I guess Paul would not agree with all this pump, but from now on, his secret childhood place would be well protected.

Someone pressed a wooden handle in my hands.

"It's your turn, Lady Byrd!" a half-mocking voice said.

I lifted my head to Ed's twinkling eyes. My dear friend could walk proudly, vested with the honor of re-discovering his remote ancestor's sacred site.

To the whoops and cheers of the small crowd, I pushed some loose earth around with the spade.

Not very efficient for a foundation, I thought, looking at my pitiful mound.

A low *whoosh* of displaced air sounded over me. I craned my neck in time to glimpse a large California Condor gliding, head like a red arrow shooting off the dark fluff of its neck, black fingers wings splayed as to grab the wind.

Ignoring the excited humans, the condor swooped down, down over us, then it passed over the cliff's edge, out of view.

Into *his* canyon.

The End

Postface: Bold and Birding

A WRITING EXERCISE directed by SF writer Dean Wesley Smith saw the birth of Lady Byrd.

Dean had asked to write a 400-word opening describing a setting that could be the most beautiful place in the world. I was inspired by a canyon picture on my computer. I didn't even got my hero or heroine's name as I typed the opening of the story. That was a bold exercice for me.

Once past the actual exercise length, I knew that woman was a widow. So she would be saddened that she couldn't share such a panorama with her husband.

❧

AS I LOVE WATCHING BIRDS, my distinguished lady character would be an avid ornithologist.

I was initiated to bird watching by my father, and remember fondly the old 1967 edition of *Birds of Canada,* with my dads' pencil annotations on the margins. I also remember the weight of the 1970's black Bushnell 7x35 binoculars, quite heavy in the hands of a child. But how many wonders it would show me! Today my powerful 15x70 Celestron composite binoculars are heavier, but not by much. My mature heroine would appreciate a lightweight daytime 9x25 binoculars.

And she would use the heavy 15x70 binos with a stand, from her balcony.

However, the fictive unnamed location was too far south from my home to watch either condor or wrens. So a helpful website was the *Cornell Lab of Ornithology* (www.allaboutbirds.org/guide/) for knowing more about the rock- and canyon wrens and to hear their haunting songs. Another helpful resource was the *Arizona-Sonora Desert Museum* (www.desertmuseum.org/books/nhsd_wrens.php) and the *National Audubon Society* (www.audubon.org/) who organise popular bird-counting activities.

❧

THE TINY WRENS survive in desertic conditions like the Sonora desert, hunting insects and spiders in crevices. A fun factoid; the male in some wren species may build several "dummy nests" before the female chooses one to lay her eggs. Hence the several "nests" in the cave's entrance.

As for the California Condor, the bird has a stunning story to tell.

Hunting and human activities chased the Condor away, until the race became almost extinct in 1987, all remaining wild individuals having been captured. With only 22 individuals left in captivity, the species was protected ans breeding programs (*California Condor Recovery Plan*) aimed at augmenting their numbers, and the California Condor has been reintroduced to northern Arizona and southern Utah (including the Grand Canyon area and Zion National Park), close to the fictive Secret Canyon.

There are still a lot of challenge, as lead poisoning from eating bullet-riddled preys kills several condors. So the Condor Watch has been formed, to help follow the birds in their journeys and social lives, to check for sins of lead behavior-altering (www.condorwatch.org/).

❧

Emboldened by my fact-finding mission, I pursued the story, digging along a precious ore vein snaking in the raw earth. Once I had finished writing and enriching it, I was caught in a conundrum: which genre was it ?

Not science fiction, of course.

As this is a realist story with an element of mystery, it could fit (loosely) inside the "cozy" category. No "murder most foul!" kind of cozy there, but my fearless bird watcher, searching for a connection with her deceased husband, discovers a problem that could endanger her fellow tourists' lives. My character had morphed into an older, more mature protagonist, quirky, fearless, at odds with the world.

Another Wonderful Odd Woman.

Like my grandma.

I had grown up with the Miss Marples and other mystery novels borrowed from my grandmother Edmée's bookshelves. At her place, my grandma and I would each read our dime paperback, in a companionable silence, me nestled on her sofa and she in her flowered armchair (which I later inherited). Edmée was an artist, and fine art painter, and I have inherited those traits from her.

So there may be some small part of her in our feisty Lady Byrd.

Michèle Laframboise

Hearfelt Thanks

My gratitude goes first to my grandmother, Edmée Laframboise (born Saintonge) for her luminous presence and inspiration.

I am indebted to my father, Jacques Laframboise, for all those wonderful hours of birdwatching. My mother, Thérèse Laframboise (born Lorrain) has always encouraged me to write.

My husband Gilles and my son Frédéric provide me their ongoing support into this writing adventure.

And to you, dear reader, for getting to the end of this mystery! If you liked that story, don't hesitate to share your impressions on your favorite platforms!

Lady Byrd will return!

About the Author

WHEN NOT TRYING to initiate first contact with strange flora, Michèle Laframboise juggles her time between drawing comics and crafting stories.

A science-fiction lover since childhood, she has published 19 novels and more than 50 short stories, earning three Auroras and two Solaris awards.

Her works have appeared in *Solaris, Carmilla, Galaxies, Géante Rouge, Brin d'Éternité, Tesseracts, Fiction River, Compelling Science Fiction,* and *Abyss&Apex*. She has been translated into French, Italian and Russian.

Holding degrees in geography and engineering, Michèle uses her scientific background to create worlds filled with humor, invention and wonder.

Official website:
www.michele-laframboise.com
in French and English

Humoristic blog:
sundayartist.wordpress.com

Publisher's website:
www.echofictions.com

Wikipedia entry: Michèle Laframboise

For some news and amusing reading reviews, join Michele's happy band of readers!

http://michele-laframboise.com/fans

Other books by Michèle

Change or die!

Science-fiction / humor / First contact

Loongunis need constant fluctuations to thrive, while the strange-haired Earthmen hate the endless unstability.

When a sabotage impairs the shift engines of their traveling Box, the enforced immobility might drive all Loongunis mad...unless their translator can work out a solution!

Science fiction adventure at its best, a quirky 7000-word story told by multiple award-winning author Michèle Laframboise.

How to Think inside the Box
978-1-988339-40-5 (print)

A lone butterfly over the Arctic...

Dystopia / Ecology / Trans-humanism

A human transplanted inside a giant monarch butterfly body roams an Earth scarred by climatic changes. He checks out pockets of survivors and reports for his industrial masters, who live in lavish palaces rolling over the Arctic synthetic ice.

The monarch is undestructible, as long as he keep to the rarefied altitudes.

But can he stay indifferent to the suffering going on under his wings?

A compelling ecological tale that has garnered the 2010 Solaris Prize and other literary accolades.

Ice Monarch

ISBN 978-1-988339-60-3 (Print)

You won't forget Malak...

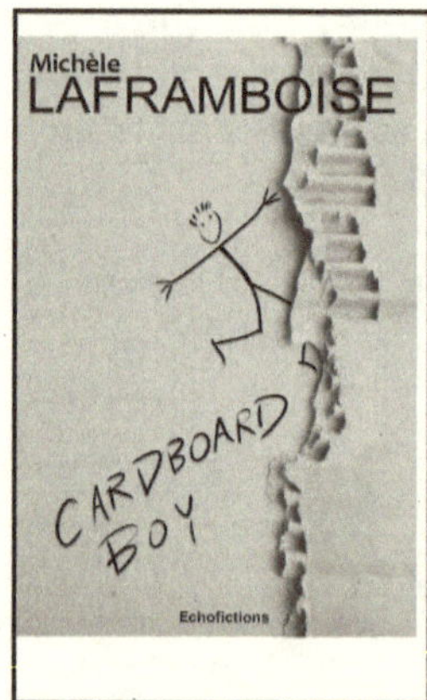

Child Labor/ Social Drama

Theo, a dispirited humanitarian, audits a child worker at a cardboard factory, in a port city somewhere in Asia. He is impressed by young Malak's maturity and grit.

When that boy, the same age as Theo's own son, disappears, he cannot let it rest. His quest for answers only raises more questions about the traps of structured help and acquired privilege.

An unsettling story quietly told by multiple awards-winning author Michèle Laframboise.

Cardboard Boy

ISBN 978-1-988339-22-1 (Print)

More on Echofictions.com/books

Friends' List

A story links every reader in a chain of friendship. Feel free to write your name before you give this book to someone close.

This is a unique feature of the printed edition!

Yearning for more stories?

Michèle Laframboise's full bibliography is enough to whet any SF reader's appetite!

michele-laframboise.com

New stories are brewing up constantly!

To get exclusive offers, curated book reviews, advanced information about coming releases, join Michele's happy band of readers!

michele-laframboise.com/fans

As a busy writer, Michèle won't send mail more often than once a month!

www.ingramcontent.com/pod-product-compliance
Lightning Source LLC
LaVergne TN
LVHW051021080826
845145LV00009B/2731

* 9 7 8 1 9 8 8 3 3 9 0 8 5 *